To our friends, Barbara and Joe, the owners of the farm.

www.mascotbooks.com

Robbie Robin

For more information, please contact:
Mascot Books
620 Herndon Parkway #320
Herndon, VA 20170
info@mascotbooks.com

Library of Congress Control Number: 2020905607

CPSIA Code: PRT0521A
ISBN-13: 978-1-64543-459-7

Printed in the United States

Robbie Robin

Theresa Perna

Illustrated by Kayla Medina

When I was a young girl, my father took our family many places during our school vacations. One of my favorites was a farm in upstate New York, where my brother, Tom, my sister, Charlotte, and I had many adventures. Dad's friend had bought a large, old farmhouse, and he was kind enough to let us visit every other weekend. My name is Mary Elizabeth, and this is one of our family stories:

the story of Robbie Robin.

In winter on the farm, we made many giant snowmen. We ice skated on the frozen pond and rode behind a snowmobile as our father pulled us on our sleds. We would drive our sled down all of the hills and drink lots of hot cocoa, which our mother always had ready for us.

In the summer, we helped weed and water the large garden. Dad's friend had planted lettuce, tomatoes, green beans, corn, squash, and eggplants. Everything was shared with our family.

We picked blueberries and blackberries and bought peaches, pears, and apples from a farmers' market. Our mother let us help make delicious applesauce, jams, pies, and breads.

We swam in a pond with the ducks, and we ran through large meadows of tall grass.

During one of our explorations, my brother, sister, best-forever-friend Andrea, and I almost stepped on a tiny baby bird. It was on the path where we were walking, and it must have fallen from its nest. It was an ugly, wrinkled little thing, and only had two fuzzy feathers on its whole body. It also had two red scratches on its back. We hurried to the house, calling for our mother to come and help us.

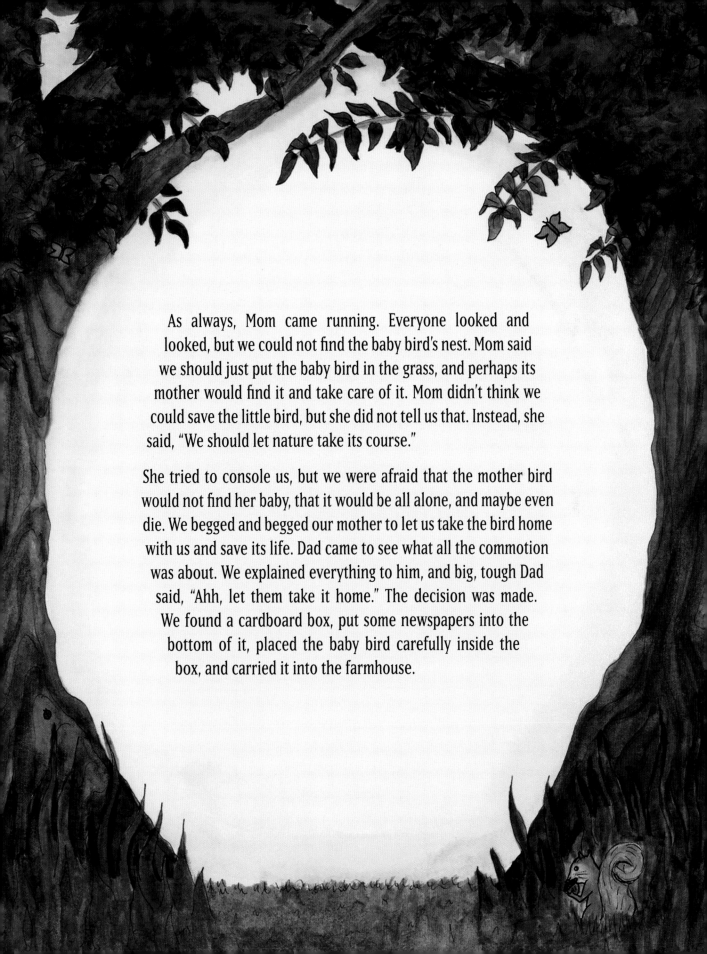

As always, Mom came running. Everyone looked and looked, but we could not find the baby bird's nest. Mom said we should just put the baby bird in the grass, and perhaps its mother would find it and take care of it. Mom didn't think we could save the little bird, but she did not tell us that. Instead, she said, "We should let nature take its course."

She tried to console us, but we were afraid that the mother bird would not find her baby, that it would be all alone, and maybe even die. We begged and begged our mother to let us take the bird home with us and save its life. Dad came to see what all the commotion was about. We explained everything to him, and big, tough Dad said, "Ahh, let them take it home." The decision was made. We found a cardboard box, put some newspapers into the bottom of it, placed the baby bird carefully inside the box, and carried it into the farmhouse.

My mother found some cotton balls, soaked them in alcohol, and swabbed the baby bird's sores on its back. It shivered in pain, but it quickly recovered. With a medicine dropper, Mom squeezed drops of water into its beak. With tweezers, she fed it some small pieces of water-soaked bread. A few hours later, we were packed into our car for the ride home. Our baby bird closed its eyes and slept, but it was also awake, saying,

"Peep,

peep,

peep,"

during much of the drive to our house.

As soon as we arrived home, Mom telephoned the Bronx Zoo and asked to speak to someone in the aviary department. Mom explained our situation and asked what to feed a baby bird. The woman on the phone told her that the baby bird had to eat every three hours, no more than that, but it needed special food.

First, we had to hard boil some eggs and save the yellow yolks. When they were cooled, we had to mash them with a certain amount of cod liver oil. Second, we had to buy canned dog food, not cat food. We had to alternate the feedings of small amounts of egg yolks one time and small amounts of dog food the next time. Of course, this had to be done with tweezers to put the food inside the little bird's beak. My mother sighed, but said, "Okay, we can do this." That baby bird was very hungry, and "peeped" its orders at us all the time!

Our pet cat, Honey, was not happy! She wanted to eat that noisy bird. No one was paying any attention to her, except to put her outside. To protect our little bird from Honey, we put it into a cardboard shoe box with holes punched in the top and sides of the box for air. Then, we placed the shoebox on the windowsill with the window open. To secure the box lid, we lowered the window gently down to hold the shoe box in place and away from Honey's reach.

In a few days, our bird became stronger and larger, and it began to grow many feathers. Soon we could see that it had the colors of a robin. We named it Robbie! We weren't sure if Robbie was a boy or a girl, but because the feathers had such bright colors, we thought it was a male bird.

When Honey was outside, we would let Robbie out of his box to walk around the kitchen. He followed our mother everywhere she went. We learned that this action is called "imprinting." Since Mom was the one who fed and nurtured him, the little animal thought Mom was his mother! Honey was scratching constantly at the outside kitchen door. She was definitely not pleased!

One day when Robbie was out of his box and on the floor behind her, my mother decided to sweep the kitchen. Her broom was long and black. Robbie became frantic, peeping loudly and sounding angry. He was afraid of the broom. Mom said that maybe it reminded him of a long black snake. Usually black snakes live around farms because they eat the mice there. Unfortunately, they also eat baby birds. We thought that perhaps it was a black snake which had knocked Robbie's nest from its tree. Mom picked up Robbie and gently rubbed his head until he calmed down. There was no more sweeping around Robbie.

Robbie grew more beautiful every day.

Mom said we had to teach him to take care of himself so he could become independent. We put Honey in the house, and we took Robbie out to the backyard, pulled up some ivy plants, and helped him find earthworms. Mom tried to feed him one with the tweezers, but it was too big for Robbie to swallow. My mother had to cut the earthworm into small pieces. She was mumbling something we could not hear, gagged a little, and had a yucky look on her face each time she cut one of those worms.

But, Robbie loved them!

My mother knew Robbie had to learn how to fly. She started putting him on her finger, lifting him off the floor, and quickly removing her finger when he was in the air. He would flap and flop to the floor, but Mom kept practicing every day. Each time she took him a little higher, until Robbie learned to fly gracefully.

As time passed, my mother explained that we could not keep Robbie. He was born to be free, not put in a birdcage. He needed to return to the place where he was born and find his family of robins. If Robbie became completely tame and stayed with us, he would probably be caught and killed by a neighborhood cat, or maybe by our Honey. We did not want that to happen. Everyone was sad, but we knew we had to let him be free. Mom asked us to be strong for Robbie's sake. "Tough love" was not easy.

In the two weeks since we had found Robbie, he had grown into a strong, beautiful bird. It was time to return him to his own home. We packed up the car that Friday afternoon, including Robbie in his box, and Dad drove us back to the farm.

We had a plan to take Robbie up the hillside, close to where we had found him, and leave him there. When we arrived at the farm, we did just that. We nestled him on the grass, found some insects and berries for him, ran as fast as we could down the hill back to the farm, and went inside without him. But Robbie had his own ideas. He followed us all the way there and was peeping loudly outside the farm door. Mom said to be very quiet and to try not to pay any attention to him.

We tiptoed into the kitchen and played some games on the table while our mother cooked dinner. Suddenly, we noticed that Robbie was chirping on the outside sill of the large kitchen window, looking at us and begging to come in. Mom said, "Be strong and ignore him." It was breaking all of our hearts, even Dad's.

Then Robbie flew away,
        and we could not see him outside.

On Saturday we did not see Robbie all morning. We did not see him all afternoon. We did not see him all evening. Our mother was really getting worried. Maybe something caught poor Robbie.

That Sunday many of our cousins visited the farm for a big family picnic. My mother prepared a large meal, and we carried everything outside to the picnic tables. Everyone was enjoying the delicious food and having many noisy conversations. My father was talking in a loud voice to one of his cousins and stood up to make an important point.

Suddenly, we were all shocked to see a robin-red-breast swoop down and land on Dad's head! Mom jumped up and cheered with tears in her eyes, and we all clapped saying,

"Robbie made it! Robbie made it!"

He flew away, and we never saw him again. Mom said that maybe Robbie had come back to let us know that he was alright and to say goodbye. I knew that Robbie leaving our "nest" made my mother feel as if one of her own children had left home. She had a very tender heart.

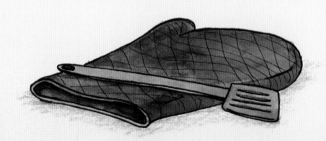

Every time we returned to the farm during the next year, we watched for Robbie, but we never saw him. We hoped he had successfully made a life with other robins. Many things happened that year. My brother, Michael, was born. Dad's friend sold the farm. Our adventures continued in other places.

For many, many years afterward, each time we saw a robin, we wondered if it was one of Robbie's children, or grandchildren, or great-grandchildren. We never forgot Robbie or the new knowledge and the smiles he gave to our family. Our mother told his story many times, and hearing about Robbie always made us a little sad . . .

but it also made us very happy.

About the Author

Theresa Perna is a retired teacher who has taught class levels from nursery school through college. She lives in Armonk, New York, with her husband of fifty-nine years. They have four children. For many years, Theresa entertained her students, children, and grandchildren with tales of family trips and adventures. This true story of Robbie Robin was a favorite, and is being published in book form at the request of her children. It is a gift to her six grandchildren.